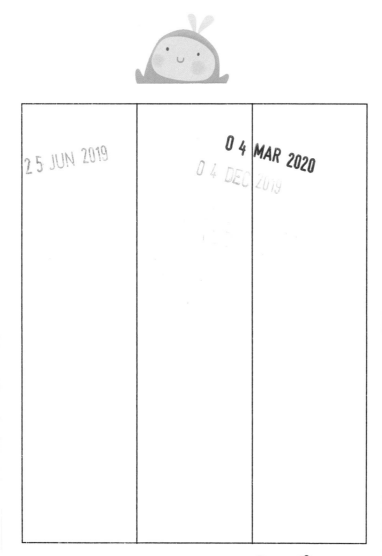

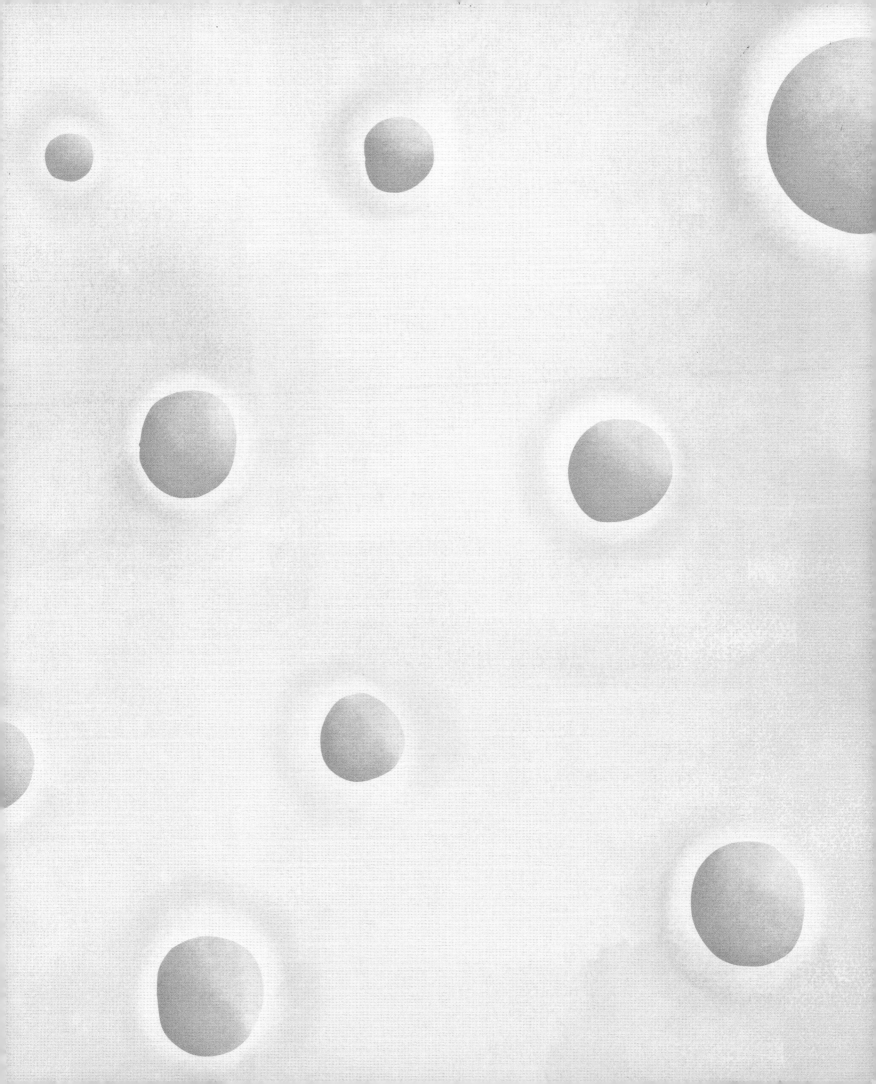

For Mum & Dad

templar
books

First published in the UK in 2019 by Templar Publishing,

an imprint of Kings Road Publishing, part of Bonnier Books UK,

The Plaza, 535 King's Road, London, SW10 0SZ

www.templarco.co.uk

www.bonnierbooks.co.uk

13 5 7 9 10 8 6 4 2

ISBN 978-1-78741-340-5

Designed by Genevieve Webster

Edited by Alison Ritchie

Printed in Malaysia

MOLLY'S MOON MISSION

DUNCAN BEEDIE

Molly the moth

lived in the back of an old wardrobe.
She loved her home and her family
but she yearned for adventure . . .

"I want to be a **real** astronaut and fly to the **Moon!**" Molly declared.
"I'm not sure your tiny wings would make it there," said her mother.

We'll see about that, thought Molly.

So when she wasn't busy helping her mum look after her siblings . . .

. . . she trained hard for her **space mission.**

Until, at long last, she was **ready!**

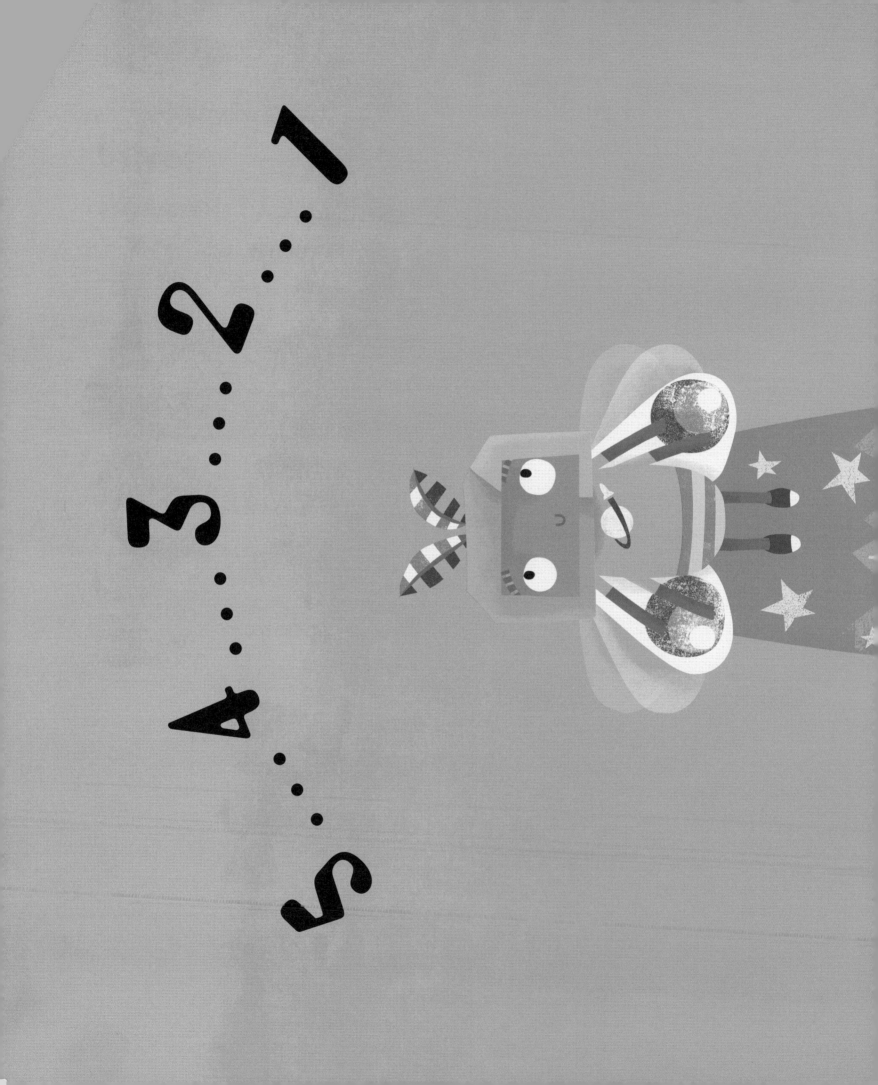

5...4...3...2...1

BLAST OFF!

And to Molly's surprise,
a few seconds later . . .

"I made it to the **Moon!**"
she cried.

"This isn't the Moon," buzzed a huge bluebottle, "This is a light bulb! The Moon is **much** bigger and **much** further away. Too far for a little mite like you."

We'll see about that,
thought Molly and she set off
in search of a much bigger light.

"So this is the Moon!"
gasped Molly.

"Oh, you poor little creature," sighed a large spider.
"This is a street lamp. The Moon is much, **much** brighter
and much, **much** further away.
Too far for a little thing like you, I'd wager!"

We'll see about that, thought Molly.
She flew on until she saw a light that was **bigger** and **brighter**
than anything she had seen before.

The closer she got, the dizzier she became,
as she followed the light round and round in circles.

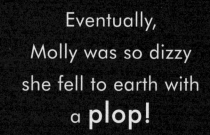

Eventually,
Molly was so dizzy
she fell to earth with
a plop!

"I guess this isn't the Moon either then," spluttered Molly.

"I'm afraid not," chuckled a wise old crab as he fished her out of the rockpool.

"This is a lighthouse. The Moon is much, **much** further away."

"Too far away for a teeny moth like me, I suppose?" Molly said sadly.

"I don't know about that," replied the crab. "I could count the number of fish
I've caught on one pincer, but it hasn't stopped me from trying night after night."

Encouraged by the crab's words, Molly patched up her helmet,
saluted, and launched herself upwards once again . . .

. . . towards the **biggest, brightest, furthest** light she could see.

But there was no one to hear her . . .

She wandered across the pale,
dusty landscape.

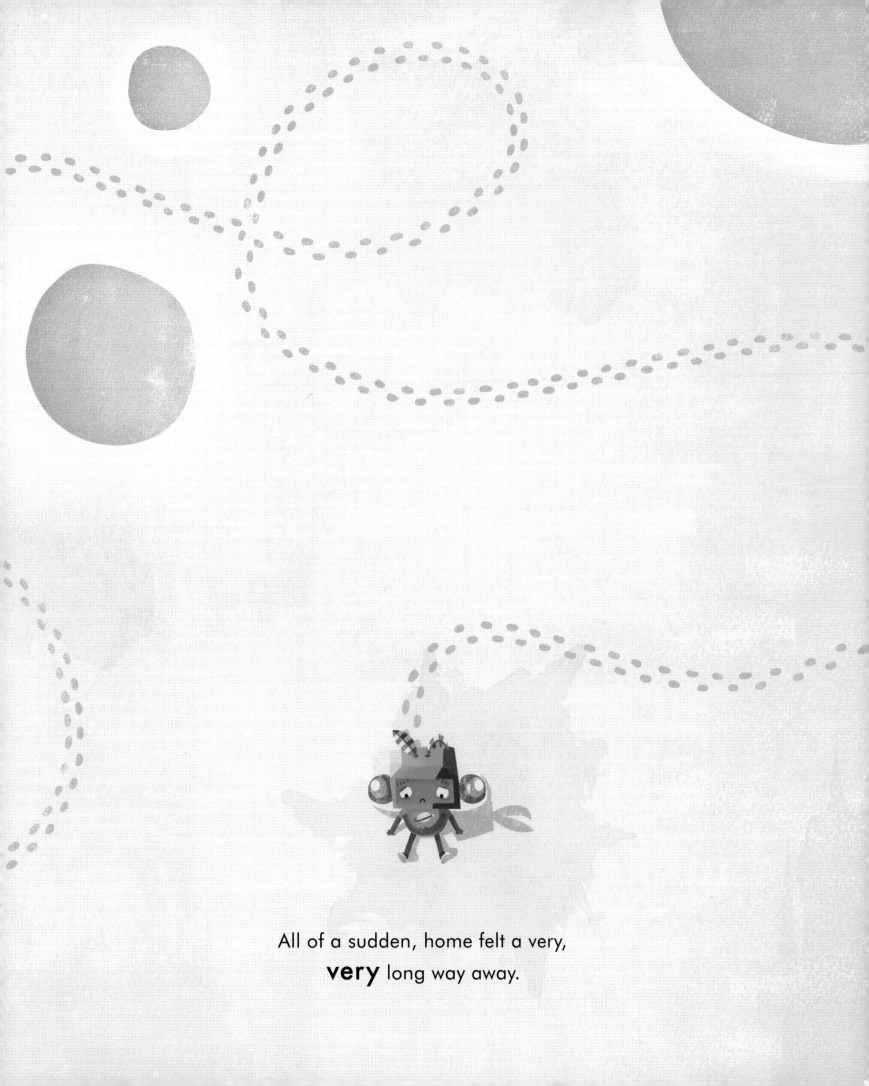

All of a sudden, home felt a very,
very long way away.

Just then, a **giant** shadow loomed over her.

ONE SMALL STEP FOR . . . A MOTH!!?

"Hey, watch out!" shrieked Molly, jumping out of the way in the nick of time. "Sorry about that, kid!" said the astronaut. "I didn't expect to find anyone else here on the Moon!"

"You mean I **actually** made it to the **Moon!**" gasped Molly. "I knew I could do it!"

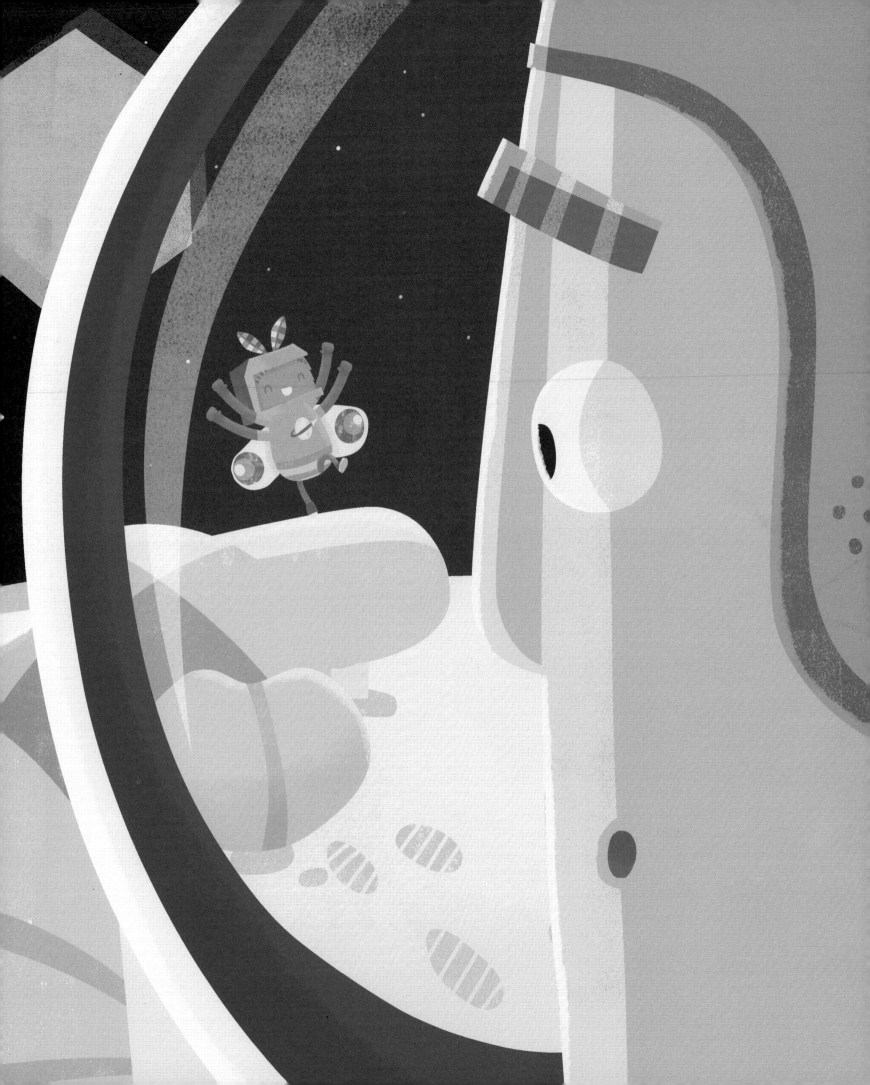

"That's a pretty **giant** leap for a little critter," said the other astronaut.
"I guess you'll be too puffed out to help us with our special mission then?"

"We'll see about that!" Molly said cheerfully.
So she helped the astronauts take photos of the Moon's surface . . .

. . . then she helped them collect samples of rocks and moon dust . . .

. . . and they even had time for some fun . . .

. . . before planting a ceremonial flag.

"We'd better be heading back," said the astronauts,
as they prepared the lunar lander for lift off.
Molly stared out into the vastness of space. It was so **dark.**
How would she ever navigate her way home?

"Cheer up! You're one of us now, kid!" the astronauts said,
and they gave Molly her very own lunar mission patch.
"Now, how about we give you a ride home?"

"Ooh, yes please!" beamed Molly.

As the astronauts busied themselves
in the module, Molly gazed out of the
window towards Earth.

Far away, the city lights twinkled.

But one of those lights was

bigger, brighter, and more inviting

than all the others.

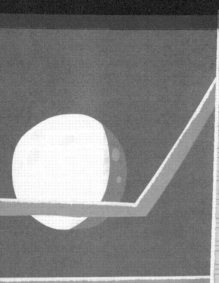

And before she knew it,
Molly was safely back home.

"I've been to the **Moon!**" Molly cried,
giving her mother a big hug.

"Well I never!" her mum exclaimed proudly.
"My Molly, the only moth ever to fly to the **Moon!**"

We'll see about that! thought Molly.

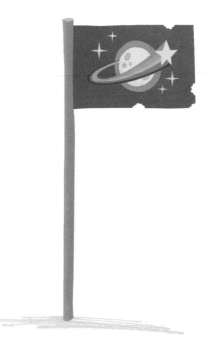

THE END

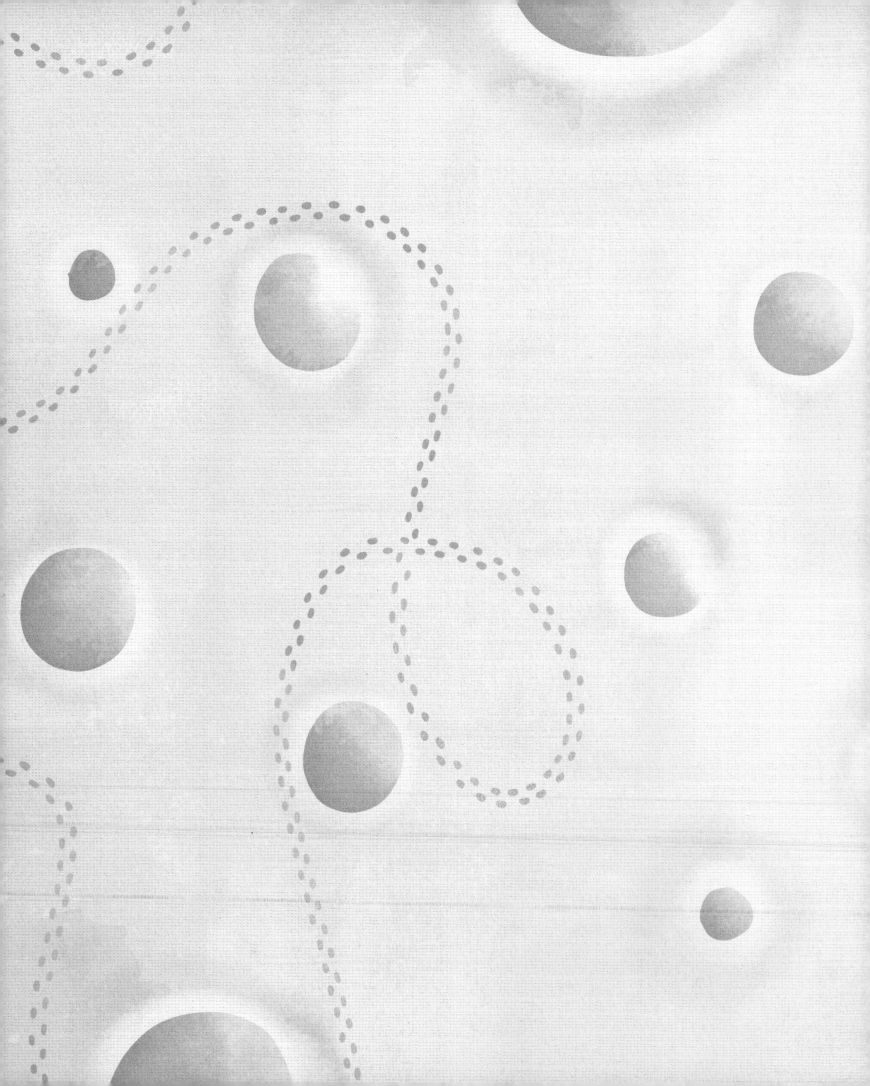